Churchill's TALE of TAILS

Anca Sandu

PEACHTREE
ATLANTA

Published by
PEACHTREE PUBLISHERS
1700 Chattahoochee Avenue
Atlanta, Georgia 30318-2112
www.peachtree-online.com

Text and illustrations © 2012 by Anca Sandu

First published in Great Britain in 2012 by Jonathan Cape,
an imprint of Random House Children's Publishers UK
First United States version published in 2014 by Peachtree Publishers
First United States trade paperback edition published in 2016

All rights reserved. No part of this publication may be reproduced, stored in a re-
trieval system, or transmitted in any form or by any means—electronic, mechanical,
photocopy, recording, or any other—except for brief quotations in printed reviews,
without the prior permission of the publisher.

The illustrations were rendered in Adobe Illustrator by combining digital color
with hand-drawn textures and shading.

Printed in July 2016 in China
10 9 8 7 6 5 4 3 2 1 (hardcover)
10 9 8 7 6 5 4 3 2 1 (trade paperback)

Library of Congress Cataloging-in-Publication Data

Sandu, Anca, author, illustrator.
 Churchill's tale of tails / by Anca Sandu.
   pages cm
 Summary: After losing his tail, Churchill the pig's friends help him search
for a new one but he becomes so caught up in how each new tail makes
him feel, he forgets his friends completely.
 ISBN 978-1-56145-738-0 (hardcover) / 978-1-56145-782-3 (trade
paperback)
 [1. Tail—Fiction. 2. Pigs—Fiction. 3. Friendship—Fiction. 4. Lost and
found possessions—Fiction.] I. Title.
 PZ7.S2217Chu 2014
 [E]—dc23
                                              2013032148

To Joe, Sue, and Abi
for believing in me
—A. S.

Churchill was a very proud pig,
just like any other pig.

This is his

TALE *of* **TAILS**.

Churchill valued many things in life:

smelling beautiful flowers,

painting self-portraits,

playing classical music,

and reading good books.

And he loved to have tea
with his friends Billy and Gruff.

But Churchill had one
thing that he prized above
everything else...

his tail.

It wasn't a big tail.

It wasn't a fancy tail.

It wasn't even a very practical tail.
But it was his tail,

and it made
him feel great.

But one morning...

his tail was nowhere to be found.

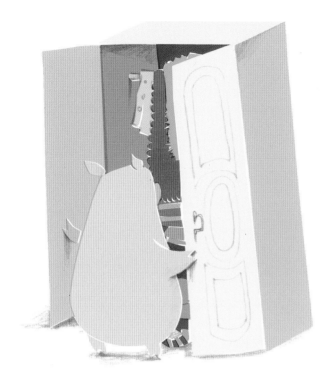

Churchill searched here,

there,

and everywhere.

Finally, he gave up searching.
He was miserable.

"I just don't feel like myself
without my tail," he said.

Billy and Gruff
came up with
a good idea.

They gave Zebra a call.

The zebras were happy to help.
They had a spare tail
for Churchill to try.

But the zebra tail didn't feel quite right.

Perhaps I should try some other tails, Churchill thought.

So he went to see Peacock.

Peacock gave Churchill a tail that made him feel beautiful.

"Ooh," said Churchill to himself. "I wonder what other tails I could try."

A tail from the fish made Churchill feel fantastic!
He could do things he'd never done before.

Churchill never talks to us anymore. It's all these fancy tails.

He tried tiny tails,

spotted tails,

snappy tails,

and tails that made him feel

big.

Trying different tails made Churchill feel so good
that he didn't have time for anything else—

not even his old friends.

Now, thought Churchill,
it's time for something very special.

So he went to Tiger's house.

Tiger's tails were really super.
"I feel fierce!" said Churchill.

"I am the world's strongest, bravest pig," he said.

"I'm not scared of anything! I'm totally fearless!" But then...

a dark shadow
fell across his path.

Eeek!

Churchill felt terrified and very alone.

What could it be?

A giant mean lizard?

An unfriendly blue alien?

Or a huge hungry robot
with a twisted fork on its head?

But it wasn't any of those things.
It was just a little bird.

"What's that on your head?"
asked Churchill. "Is it my tail?"

"Well, I don't know," the bird replied. "I found it in a bush.

I thought it
was a worm,

but I couldn't eat it.

It didn't look like a flower.

It was useless.
So I put it
on my head.
I've grown
rather fond
of it."

"Oh, but it is my
very own perfect tail,"
said Churchill.
"Please may I have
it back?"

"Well," said Bird, "if it's yours then you should have it!"
"Thank you," said Churchill.

Finding his old tail made Churchill
feel like his old self again.
He was so grateful that he
helped Bird find the perfect
thing for her head.

And making a kind new friend
helped Churchill remember his old ones.

So he organized a tea party to bring all his friends
together. "My dear friends," said Churchill,
"I have been a very silly pig, and a very bad
friend. Can you ever forgive me?"

And they did, because they loved Churchill
(even though he could be very silly).
From then on, Churchill took great care
of his own perfect tail,

and he was perfectly happy with it...

most of the time.